HERE IS THE

RHINOCEROS TAP

BOOK & RECORDING SET

painstakingly

REDESIGNED, REFORMATTED,
REVISED, RECOLORED, REMASTERED,
RESEQUENCED, AND RERELEASED

Though just now it occurs to us
that maybe it was actually just fine the way it was.
But oh well.

DELUXE ILLUSTRATED LYRICS BOOK

RHINOCEROS TAP

LYRICS *and* DRAWINGS *by* SANDRA BOYNTON

MUSIC *by* MICHAEL FORD & SANDRA BOYNTON

WORKMAN PUBLISHING · NEW YORK

FOR OUR FAMILIES, OF COURSE:

Jamie, Caitlin, Keith, Devin, and Darcy — *S. B.*

Beth, Rachel, John, and Katie — *M. F.*

Lisa and Matt — *A. B.*

"Barnyard Dance" is based on Sandra Boynton's board book published by Workman Publishing • "Horn to Toes" is based on Sandra Boynton's board book published by Simon & Schuster

Library of Congress Cataloging-in-Publication Data on file

WORKMAN PUBLISHING COMPANY, INC., 225 VARICK STREET, NEW YORK, NY 10014-4381 WWW.WORKMAN.COM WWW.SANDRABOYNTON.COM
PRINTED IN CHINA. FIRST PRINTING: MARCH 2004

CONTENTS

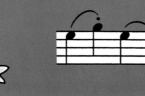

LOOK AS YOU LISTEN

SONG # 1

INTRODUCTION

I have to tell you I know
a ballerina rhino
whose pirouettes would make you
smile and clap.
But though ballet is pretty,
it seems to me a pity
that she doesn't learn to do......

PLEASE
TURN THE
PAGE

Hit it, Max! →

As soon as my friends hear that tappy-tap sound, they hurry to join me from miles around.
The cows and the piggies, the buffalo twins, start hoofing in time when the chorus begins.

SONG #

1

(continued)

The Rhinoceros Tap

Tippy dum. Dum. Dum. Dum. Tippy dum. Dum. Dum. Dum…

Whenever I'm lonesome, whenever I'm blue,
whenever I'm worried, I know what to do—
I put on my tap shoes, I wear my best clothes,
I start up the music, and here's how it goes:

Rhinoceros Tap, Rhinoceros Tap,
first you do two shuffles then you flap, flap, flap.
You dig with your heel and you spank with your toe
and when you pitter patter, you can really let go—

SKITTERY CAT, SKITTERY CAT, *STOMP STOMP!*
RABBITTY RABBITTY RABBITTY RABBITTY, SKITTERY CAT, *STOMP!*

FOR MUSIC & ALL LYRICS, PLEASE TURN TO PAGE 43

I can't leave my place till the peas are all gone. At the rate I am going, I'll be ninety-one.

O, Lonely Peas

Dinner is over.
I like what I ate.
Except for the peas,
which are still on my plate.

*O, Lonely Peas,
so green, so round,
and so small.
O, Lonely Peas,
there's no one
who loves you at all.
There's no one
who loves you at all.*

I can't leave my place
till the peas are all gone.
At the rate I am going,
I'll be ninety-one.

*O, Lonely Peas,
so green, so round, and so small.
O, Lonely Peas,
there's no one who loves you at all.
No, no one who loves you at all.*

Perhaps by some magic,
they'll all disappear—
★ A B R A C A D A B R A !

...The peas are still here.

FOR MUSIC & ALL LYRICS, PLEASE TURN TO PAGE 44

They never ever do the things that they should. Oh, Bad Babies, why can't you be good?

Bad Babies

I'm five years old, so you can take it from me—
these babies are never what you want them to be.
They whine and they bite, they chew on your toys,
and oh! do they make the most terrible noise!

I tell you: *Bad Babies, they yell and they cry.*
Bad, Bad Babies—you never know why.
They never ever do the things that they should.
Oh, Bad Babies, why can't you be good?

Wherever they go, it's always a mess.
They only yell **NO.** They never say YES.
I can't even hear what I'm trying to say
with all those babies being bad all day.

I'm saying: *Bad Babies, they yell and they cry.*
Bad, Bad Babies—you never know why.
They never ever do the things that they should.
Oh, Bad Babies, why can't you be good?

(Aw, now look what you did...)

FOR MUSIC
& ALL LYRICS,
PLEASE TURN
TO PAGE 45

HEY! what a HEY! what a HEY! what a **CRAB!** *Heigh-ho crabby crabby, ho ho, crab!*

SONG # 4

The Crabby Song

QUARTET: **S**ailors love to sail the seas in weather bad or fair.
They love to feel the ocean breeze
and sniff the salty air.
They love to laugh.
They love to work.
They love to eat good food...

CAPTAIN:

This is your captain speaking! Cut out that singing!
Get back to work!

QUARTET: ...They love to sing you this fine song
when you're in a terrible mood:

Hey, what a crab and a Ho, what a crab!
Hey, what a crab and a Ho, what a crab!
HEY! what a HEY! what a
HEY! what a **CRAB!**
Heigh-ho crabby crabby, ho ho, crab!

FOR MUSIC & ALL LYRICS, PLEASE TURN TO PAGE 46

Ba-doo-ba-doink, doink, SNUFFLE DEE DAH. Ba-doo-ba-doink, doink, PIGGY DOO WAH.
Ba-doo-ba-doink, doink, SNUFFLE DEE DAH. Ba-doo-ba-Chattanooga piggy piggy piggily dee...

SONG # 5

Perfect Piggies

Did you ever see noses so wonderfully round?
Where else could these curly little tails be found?
From the spring of our tail to our snuffling snout,
our plumpness is pleasing, there isn't a doubt.
And look at these ears, so floppy and fine.
You have to admit it—we're fabulous swine!

*We are all perfect piggies
and we know what we need.
It's really very simple,
very simple indeed:
a troughful of food,
a place in the sun,
and a little bit of comfort
when the day is done.*

FOR MUSIC & ALL LYRICS, PLEASE TURN TO PAGE 47

You tell me the islands are very very pretty,
but me, I find them…a little too gritty.

SONG # 6

Tropical Sand

(Okay, guys. Ready? Let's go, man.)

You like Hawaii
where the oceans roar.
You like Bermuda
with the pink, pink shore.
You like Aruba
where the palm trees sway.
You like Montego
with its beautiful bay.
You like the tropical sun
and the tropical sea.
But hey, mon,
Alaska sounds good to me.

I got the sand in my toes
and the sand in my nose,
the sand in my ears
and the sand in my clothes.

I got the sand in my hair
and the sand in my face.
I think I got the sand
most every place.

You like the tropical birds
in their tropical flight.
I get the tropical bugs
with their tropical bite.
You like to be playing
in the sun when it's hot.
I wish I could find me
some shade where it's not.
You tell me the islands
are very very pretty,
but me, I find them...
a little too gritty.

FOR MUSIC & ALL LYRICS, PLEASE TURN TO PAGE 48

I'm looking for something. I don't know what. So starting today, I'm a traveling mutt.

SONG # 7

So Long, Doggies

So long and farewell to my puppy dog friends.
We've had some good times, but here's where it ends.
I don't want to chase rabbits, and I don't want to play.
I just came here to tell you that I'm going away.
We've been running in circles. Enough is enough.
Staying around is just ruff, ruff, ruff.

So long, doggies—doggies, good-bye.
I'm going away, and I'm telling you why:
I'm tired of barking up the wrong, wrong tree.
I've got places to go, and places to see,
and that's why
I'm saying so long, doggies, good-bye.

FOR MUSIC & ALL LYRICS, PLEASE TURN TO PAGE 49

SONG #
8

The Shortest Son

Short, short. So short.
Short, short. So short…

g in the Universe

The shortest song in the universe
really isn't much fun.
It only has ONE…puny verse.
And now it's done.

(Ho!)

Oh, what a gyp, gyp—oh, what a gyp, gyp.
Oh, what a gyp, gyp—oh, what a gyp, gyp.
Short, short. So short. Short, short. So short…

FOR MUSIC, PLEASE TURN TO PAGE 50

And we have a fuzzy TUMMY that we all like to pat
and a little BELLY BUTTON in the middle of that.

Horns to Toes

Oh, we've each got these **HORNS** right on top of our **HEAD**
and we've each got two **EARS** so we can hear what you said,
and we've all got a **MOUTH** so we can eat, sing, or talk
and we've all got two **FEET** so we can go for a walk.

From our horns to toes,
that's exactly how it goes.
You gotta have your highs and lows—
We're happy from our horns to toes.

Yes, we've each got ten **TOES** and we've each got one **NOSE**
and we've each got two **EYES** that we can open and close,
and we have a fuzzy **TUMMY** that we all like to pat
and a little **BELLY BUTTON** in the middle of that.

From our horns to toes,
that's exactly how it goes.
You gotta have your highs and lows—
We're happy from our horns to toes.

FOR MUSIC & ALL LYRICS, PLEASE TURN TO PAGE 51

*STOMP YOUR FEET! CLAP YOUR HANDS! EVERYBODY READY FOR A **BARNYARD DANCE**!*

Barnyard Dance

*STOMP YOUR FEET! CLAP YOUR HANDS!
EVERYBODY READY FOR A BARNYARD DANCE!*

Bow to the horse.
Bow to the cow.
Twirl with the pig
if you know how.
Bounce with the bunny.
Strut with the duck.
Spin with the chickens now—
CLUCK CLUCK CLUCK!

*With a BAA and a MOO
and a COCKADOODLEDOO,
everybody promenade,
two by two!*

Prance with the horses,
skitter with the mice.
Swing with your partner
once or twice.
Stand with the donkey.
Slide with the sheep.
Scramble with the little chicks—
CHEEP CHEEP CHEEP!

*With a NEIGH and a MOO
and a COCKADOODLEDOO,
everybody promenade,
two by two!*

FOR MUSIC
& ALL LYRICS,
PLEASE TURN
TO PAGE 52

I love you more than cheese, my dear. I have no need of food.

I Love You More Than Cheese

I've been trying to think how to tell you just what you mean to me.
By now I know very well you are all that a mouse should be:
Your little pink ears, your quivering nose—for me there could be no other.
So here is the song that I'd like to propose,
one mouse to another:

I love you more than cheese,
my dear.
A Liederkranz won't do.
Mere Roquefort wouldn't please,
my pet,
if I could be with you.

I love you more than cheese,
my dear.
I have no need of food—
no Goudas, Muensters, Bries,
my love,
I'm just not in the mood.

I'd give up Provolone
if you would have it so.
If you'd give me a
kiss, please,
then Swiss cheese
I'd forego.

Of Philadelphia Cream
I need no longer dream,
for I love you more
than cheese.

FOR MUSIC,
PLEASE TURN
TO PAGE 53

If you're feeling blue and you don't know what to do,
there is nothing like a Tickle Time to make you feel like new.

SONG #
12

Tickle Time

LOW GUY: Gitchy-gitchy goo, gotta gitchy-gitchy goo, gotta gitchy-gitchy goo, gotta...

SECOND GUY: GOO GOO GITCHY-GITCHY, GOO GOO GITCHY-GITCHY...

HIGH GUYS: *Tickle Time, Tickle Time, tickle-tickle-tickle-tickle. Tickle Time, Tickle Time, tickle-tickle-tickle-tickle, gitchy-gitchy GIGGLE gitchy* **STOP STOP STOP!**

Okay. Go.

LOW GUY: Gitchy-gitchy goo, gotta gitchy-gitchy goo...

If you're feeling blue
and you don't know what to do,
there is nothing like a Tickle Time
to make you feel like new.
Oh, there's nothing like a Tickle Time
to make you feel like new,
so let's all get together
and we'll gitchy-gitchy goo.

(Goo bop. Gitchy goo bop.)

FOR MUSIC, & ALL LYRICS, PLEASE TURN TO PAGE 54

How can I feed this dinosaur
who eats my lunch and asks for more?

SONG #
13

Dinosaur Round

How can I feed this dinosaur
who eats my lunch and asks for more?

"MORE! MORE! MORE! MORE!"

Never own a dinosaur.

{REPEAT.}

FOR MUSIC,
PLEASE TURN
TO PAGE 55

I love your **WINGS.** (DUM, DUM) *I love your* **BEAK.** (DUM, DUM)
You do those **THINGS.** (DUH-DUM, DUH-DUM) *They're so* **UNIQUE.** (DUM, DUM)

SONG # 14

Turkey Love Song

Hey there! You're a chicken. And I'm a turkey. And here is my love song just to you:

I love your **WINGS.** *(dum, dum)*
I love your **BEAK.** *(dum, dum)*
You do those **THINGS.** *(duh-DUM, duh-DUM)*
They're so **UNIQUE.** *(dum, dum)*

I love your **EYES.** *(dum, dum)*
The way you **WALK.** *(dum, dum)*
I love your **VOICE.** *(duh-DUM, duh-DUM)*
The way you **SQUAWK.** *(dum, dum)*

I'm so **ALONE.** *(dum, dum)*
Alone and **BLUE.** *(dum, dum)*
Come be my **OWN.** *(duh-DUM, duh-DUM)*
And love me, **TOO.** *(dum, dum)*

You need to **KNOW** *(dum, dum)*
about my **LOVE.** *(dum, dum)*
Hey! Where'd you **GO** *(duh-DUM, duh-DUM)*
my turkey **DOVE?** *(dum, dum)*
Hey! Where'd you **GO** *(duh-DUM, duh-DUM)*
my turkey **DOVE?** *(dum, dum)*

Well, how do you like that?
Another one flies the coop.
Okay, she's not the
only bird on this farm...
Ahaaa!

FOR MUSIC & ALL LYRICS, PLEASE TURN TO PAGE 56

Little One, Little One, nighttime is nearing. Little One, Little One, it's time for sleep.

Little One

Little One, Little One, nighttime is nearing.
Little One, Little One, it's time for sleep.
Little One, Little One, stars are appearing—
silver and gold in the silent and deep.

*The roll of the river,
the song of the sea,
the hush of the darkening sky,
the rustling forest,
the whispering wind,
the sound of a soft lullaby
for my*

Little One, Little One. Come, let me hold you.
Little One, Little One, come here with me.
Little One, Little One, haven't I told you
you're the best Little One
ever could be?

FOR MUSIC,
PLEASE TURN
TO PAGE 57

PART TWO

SING & PLAY ALONG

Rhinoceros Tap

Whenever I'm lonesome,
whenever I'm blue,
whenever I'm worried,
I know what to do—
I put on my tap shoes,
I wear my best clothes,
I start up the music
and here's how it goes:
    [CHORUS]
As soon as my friends hear
that tappy-tap sound,
they hurry to join me
from miles around.

The cows and the piggies,
the buffalo twins,
start hoofing in time when the
chorus begins.
(Take it, Maudie!)
Dooby WAH, WAH, WAH, WAH.
Dooby WAH, WAH, WAH, WAH...
    [CHORUS]
Skittery cat. Skittery cat.
Skittery cat. *(STOMP! STOMP!)*
Rabbity hop. Rabbity,
rabbity, skittery cat. Stomp.
(Oh, yeah! Ha! OOO!

Look at us!)
It's getting near midnight,
the music goes on.
My friends are asleep,
but I'll dance until dawn.
So please won't you join me?
The moon is still bright.
Our feet can be happy,
our hearts can be light.
*(Let's close it down
to a whisper.)*
Putta SKISS SKISS SKISS SKISS,
Putta SKISS SKISS SKISS SKISS...

Rhinoceros Tap,
Rhinoceros Tap,
First you do two shuffles
then you flap flap flap.
You scuff with your heel
and you brush with your toe.
You don't have to pitter patter.
You can just go slow—
PUPPY DOG ONE. PUPPY DOG TWO.
PUPPY DOG THREE. *SHH, SHH!*
RABBITY SLEEP, RABBITY SLEEP.
SLUMBER IN TIME.
(That's all. Oh, yeah.)

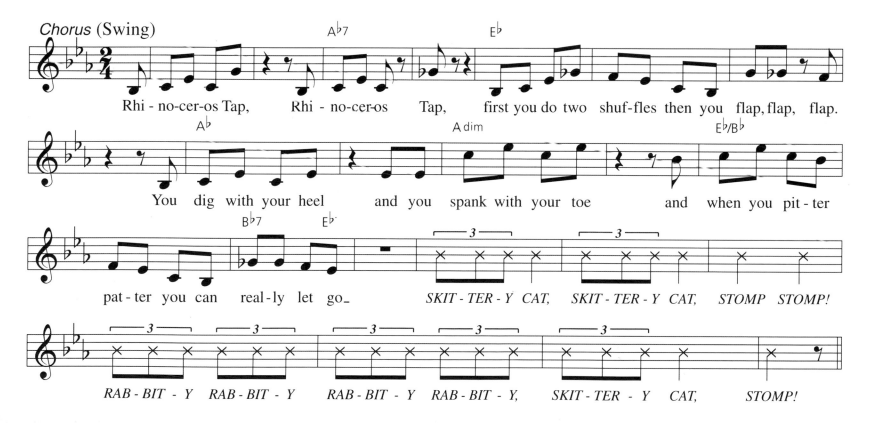

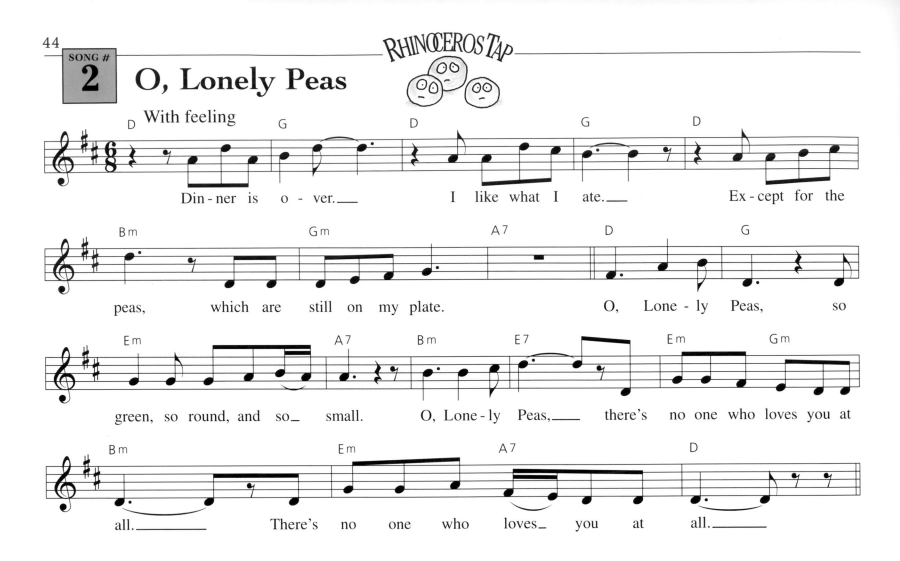

2 O, Lonely Peas

With feeling

Din - ner is o - ver.___ I like what I ate.___ Ex - cept for the

peas, which are still on my plate. O, Lone - ly Peas, so

green, so round, and so_ small. O, Lone - ly Peas,___ there's no one who loves you at

all._____ There's no one who loves_ you at all._____

I can't leave my place till the peas are all gone.
At the rate I am going, I'll be ninety-one.

O, Lonely Peas, so green, so round, and so small.
O, Lonely Peas, there's no one who loves you at all.
No, no one who loves you at all.

Perhaps by some magic, they'll all disappear—
ABRACADABRA!...The peas are still here.

(*Sing along with me, Peas!*)

O, Lonely Peas, so green, so round, and so small.
O, Lonely Peas, there's no one who loves you at all.

I'm growing quite fond of these peas of my own.
So how could I eat them? I'd be all alone. OH!
O, Lonely Peas, so green, so round, and so small.
O, Lonely Peas...there's no one. I know there is no one.
There surely is no one—there's no one who loves you
at all.

(Now help me out here—)

Bad Babies

Irritably

I'm five years old, so you can take it from me: these ba-bies are nev-er what you want them to be._ They

whine and they bite, they chew on your toys, and oh! do they make the most ter-ri-ble noise! I tell you:

Bad Ba-bies, they yell and they cry.__ Bad, Bad Ba-bies, you nev-er know why. They

nev-er ev-er do the things that they should. Oh, Bad Ba-bies, why can't you be good?_____

Wherever they go, it's always a mess.
They only yell **NO.** They never say YES.
I can't even hear what I'm trying to say
with all those babies being bad all day.
  I'm saying:
Bad Babies, they yell and they cry.
Bad, Bad Babies—you never know why.
They never ever do the things that they should.
Oh, Bad Babies, why can't you be good?
  (Aw, now look what you did...)

But maybe maybe maybe in a year or three
these babies so bad will be as good as me.
Yes, maybe maybe maybe if we all get along,
I'll teach them to sing the Bad Baby song.
  It goes:
Bad Babies, they yell and they cry.
Bad, Bad Babies—you never know why.
They never ever do the things that they should.
Oh, Bad Babies...
  (You're on, Babies):

Bad Babies, they yell and they cry.
Bad, Bad Babies—you never know why.
They never ever do
the things that they should.
Oh, Bad Babies,
    Why can't you be good?
why can't you be good?
  (Put that down. Oh, yuck!
  Stop that crying.
  You're so bad.)

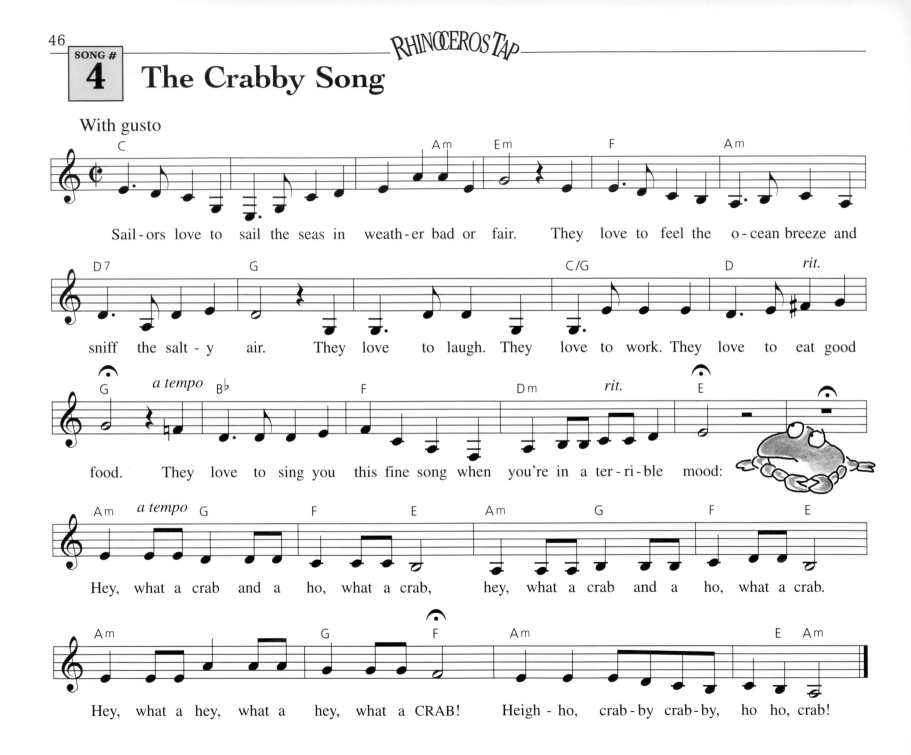

Perfect Piggies

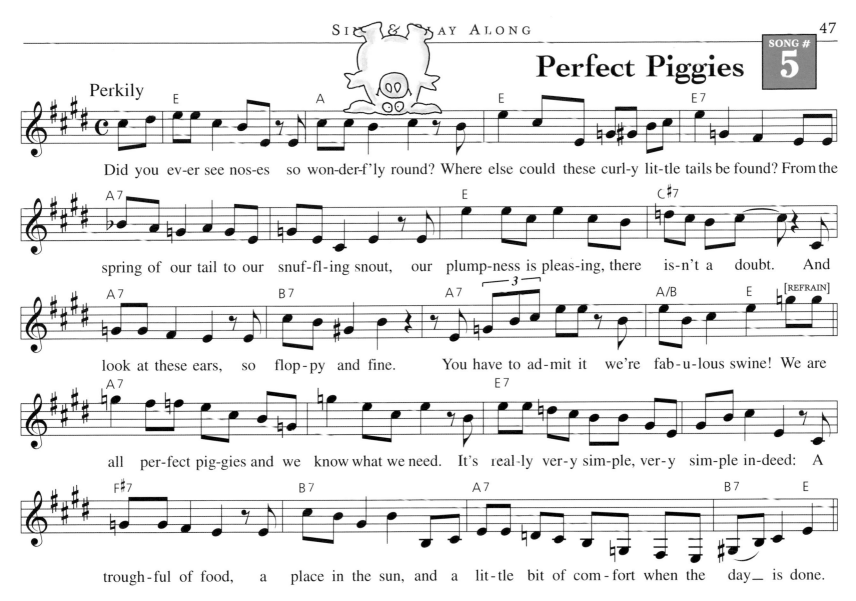

Perkily

Did you ev-er see nos-es so won-der-f'ly round? Where else could these curl-y lit-tle tails be found? From the spring of our tail to our snuf-fl-ing snout, our plump-ness is pleas-ing, there is-n't a doubt. And look at these ears, so flop-py and fine. You have to ad-mit it we're fab-u-lous swine! We are all per-fect pig-gies and we know what we need. It's real-ly ver-y sim-ple, ver-y sim-ple in-deed: A trough-ful of food, a place in the sun, and a lit-tle bit of com-fort when the day__ is done.

Ba-doo-ba-doink, doink, SNUFFLE DEE DAH.
Ba-doo-ba-doink, doink, PIGGY DOO WAH...
Now, a piggy needs kindness.
A piggy needs care.
A piggy needs to frolic in the open air.
A piggy needs hope, yes,
and now and again,
a piggy needs time in a piggy's own pen.
We really don't ask to be greatly admired.
We just want to lie down
when our trotters get tired.   [REFRAIN]

NOW SOME HAVE MORE WIT.
SOME HAVE MORE STYLE.
But no one around has a lovelier smile.
SOME LIKE TO WORK.
SOME LIKE TO THINK.
Piggies are born to be chubby and pink.
Now a pig is a pig and that's
how it should be—
You have to be you, we have to be we.
We go: *WEE WEE WEE*, all the way home.

All the way home. All the way home.
These little piggies go *WEE WEE WEE.*
All the way home.
These little piggies go *WEE WEE WEE.*
All the way home. All the way home. All the way home.
These little piggies go *WEE WEE WEE.*
All the way home. All the way home.
All the way home. All the way home.
All the way home.
THESE LITTLE PIGGIES GO PIGGLEDY BOP.

RHINOCEROS TAP

SONG # 6

Tropical Sand

(Okay, guys. Ready? Let's go, man.)

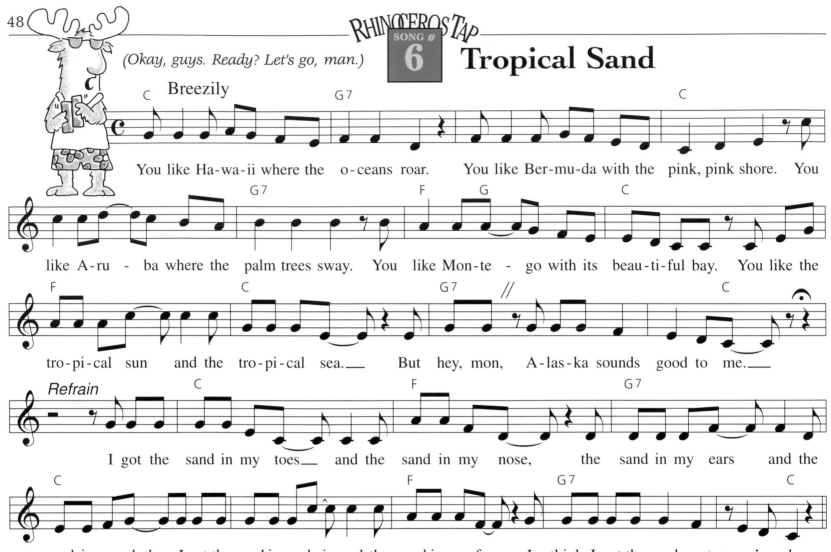

You like the tropical birds in their tropical flight.
I get the tropical bugs with their tropical bite.
You like to be playing in the sun when it's hot.
I wish I could find me some shade where it's not.
You tell me the islands are very very pretty,
but me, I find them…a little too gritty.

[REFRAIN]

You spend the whole day by the turquoise sea;
at night time, the beach comes home with me.
I got the sand in my bed, and I think very soon
I'll be trying to sleep in my own sand dune.
When Sandman comes to put the sand in my eyes,
that little man is in for a big surprise:

[REFRAIN]

I just want to go.
I don't like the sand.
I want to see snow.
Or green green land.
When the next boat
comes to Montego Bay,
Jamaica, farewell.
I'll be on my way.

So Long, Doggies

So long and farewell to my puppy dog friends.
We've had some good times, but here's where it ends.
I don't want to chase rabbits, and I don't want to play.
I just came here to tell you that I'm going away.
We've been running in circles. Enough is enough.
Staying around is just ruff, ruff, ruff.

Refrain

So long, dog-gies_ dog-gies, good-bye. I'm go-ing a-way, and I'm tell-ing you why: I'm

tired of bark-ing up the wrong, wrong tree. I've got pla-ces to go,_ and

pla-ces to see._ And that's why I'm say-ing so long, dog-gies, good-bye.

Oh, why do you hound dogs just howl at the moon?
I'm leaving today, and I'm changing my tune.
I'm looking for something. I don't know what.
So starting today, I'm a traveling mutt.
I've got to move on, for it's sad but it's true—
I'm six years old, but I feel forty-two.

[REFRAIN]

AH, YOU CAN'T HAVE RESPECT FOR A DOG THAT BEGS.
A DOG NEEDS TO STAND ON ITS OWN FOUR LEGS.
I'M NOT LOOKING FOR SOMEONE TO THROW ME A BONE.
I'M MY OWN DOG NOW, I CAN MAKE IT ALONE.

Well, I'm leaving my collar. I'm leaving my tags.
I'm bringing a dream and a tail that wags.

My heart is warm and my nose is still cold,
I want to get around before I grow too old.
I'm taking my leave, and I'm showing you how:
When you make an exit, take a bow wow wow.
Oh, so long, doggies—doggies, good-bye.
I'm going away, and I'm telling you why:
I'm tired of barking up the wrong, wrong tree.
I've got places to go, and places to see…
I'm a lone dog rover, and I have to run free.
I'm my own dog rover. I belong to me.
No digging through cans. I've got bigger plans.
No garbàge. Bone voyage. So long.
Dog gone.

SONG #
8

RHINOCEROS TAP

The Shortest Song in the Universe

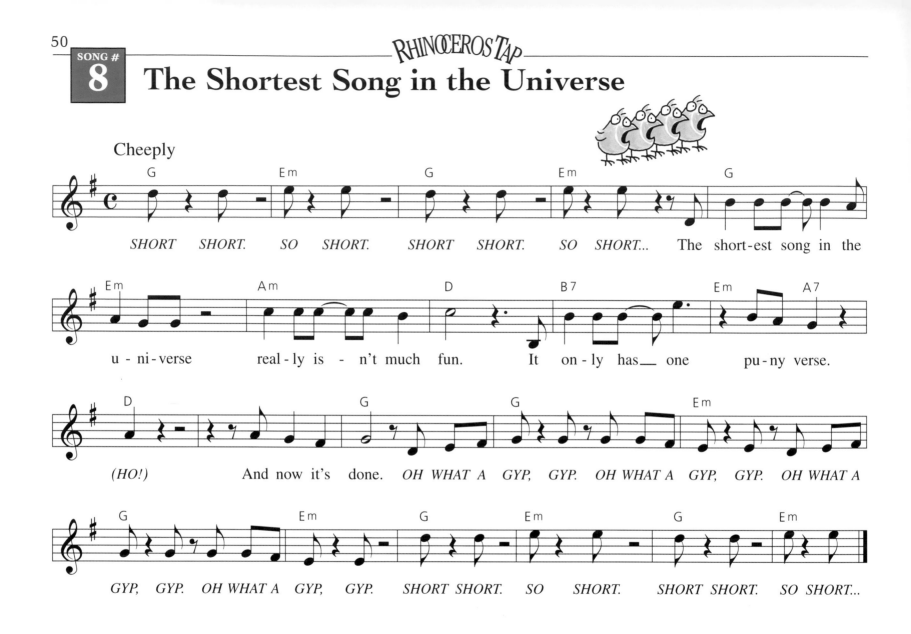

Cheeply

SHORT SHORT. SO SHORT. SHORT SHORT. SO SHORT... The short-est song in the

u - ni-verse real-ly is - n't much fun. It on-ly has___ one pu-ny verse.

(HO!) And now it's done. *OH WHAT A GYP, GYP. OH WHAT A GYP, GYP. OH WHAT A*

GYP, GYP. OH WHAT A GYP, GYP. SHORT SHORT. SO SHORT. SHORT SHORT. SO SHORT...

Horns to Toes

With whatever it takes

Oh, we've each got these HORNS right on top of our HEAD and we've each got two EARS so we can hear what you said, and we've all got a MOUTH so we can eat, sing, or talk and we've all got two FEET so we can go for a walk. From our horns to toes, that's ex-act-ly how it goes. You got-ta have your highs and lows. We're hap-py from our horns to toes.__

Yes, we've each got ten TOES
and we've each got one NOSE
and we've each got two EYES
that we can open and close,
and we have a fuzzy TUMMY
that we all like to pat
and a little BELLY BUTTON
in the middle of that.
From our horns to toes,
that's exactly how it goes.
You gotta have your highs and lows—
We're happy from our horns to toes.

WELL, WE'VE EACH GOT A BACK
AND A TAIL THAT IS LONG
AND TWO VERY FINE ARMS
AND TWO LEGS THAT ARE STRONG!
WE'VE GOT TWO HANDY HANDS
AND OUR FINGERS COUNT TEN.
WE CAN TICKLE, TICKLE, TICKLE
OR JUST COUNT THEM AGAIN—
Horns to toes!
Horns to toes!
YOU SEE OUR TEETH WHEN WE GRIN.
YOU SEE OUR TONGUES WHEN IT'S HOT.

YOU CAN WATCH US SHAKE & SHIMMY
WITH WHATEVER WE GOT!
We've got:
Horns to toes.
That's exactly how it goes.
You gotta have your highs and lows—
We're happy from our horns to toes.
You got your highs and lows—
We're happy from our horns to toes.
You gotta have your highs and lows—
Happy from our horns to toes.

YES!

SONG # 10

Barnyard Dance

STOMP YOUR FEET! CLAP YOUR HANDS!
EVERYBODY READY FOR A BARNYARD DANCE!

Squarely

Bow to the horse. Bow to the cow. Twirl with the pig if you know how.

Bounce with the bun-ny. Strut with the duck. Spin with the chick-ens now, CLUCK CLUCK CLUCK!

With a BAA and a MOO and a COCK-A-DOO-DLE - DOO,___ ev-'ry-bod-y prom-e-nade, two by two!

Prance with the horses,
skitter with the mice.
Swing with your partner
once or twice.
Stand with the donkey.
Slide with the sheep.
Scramble with the little chicks—
CHEEP CHEEP CHEEP!

*With a NEIGH and a MOO
and a COCKADOODLEDOO,
everybody promenade, two by two!*

That promenade is pretty as can be—
Go all around the barn, then home to me.
(Step lively, folks. All right. Lookin' real nice.
Now that's what I call Agri-Culture.)

Now trot with the turkey, leap with the frog.
Take another spin with the barnyard dog.
Turn with the cow in a patch of clover.
All take a bow, and the dance is over.

*With an OINK and a MOO and a
QUACK QUACK QUACK,
the dance is done, but we'll be back!*

I Love You More Than Cheese

With a little whine

I love you more than cheese, my dear. A Lied-er-kranz won't do. Mere

Roque-fort would-n't please, my pet, if I could be with you. I love you more than cheese, my dear, I

have no need of food. No Gou-das, Muen-sters, Bries, my love, I'm just not in the mood. I'd

give up Pro-vo-lo-ne if you would have it so. If you'd give me a kiss, please, then Swiss cheese I'd fore-

go. Of Phil-a-del-phia Cream I need no long-er dream, for I love you more than cheese.___

SONG # 12 Tickle Time

Relentlessly

If you're feel-ing blue and you don't know what to do, there is noth-ing like a Tick-le Time to

make you feel like new. Oh, there's noth-ing like a Tick-le Time to make you feel like new, so

let's all get to-geth-er and we'll gitch-y gitch-y goo. GOO BOP. GITCH-Y GOO BOP.

GOO BOP. GITCHY GOO BOP...
GITCHY-GITCHY GOO, GITCHY GOO.
We can tickle left.
We can tickle right.
We can tickle all the day
until the tickle night.
Tickle UP.
Tickle DOWN.
Tickle all around the town.
Tickle HIGH.
Tickle LOW.
Tickle
QUICKQUICKQUICKQUICKQUICK!
Tickle S. L. O...
Double-double u, need a double-W.
Need a gitchy-gitchy goo, gotta gitchy-gitchy goo...

If you're feeling blue
and you don't know what to do,
there is nothing like a Tickle Time
to make you feel like new.
Oh, there's nothing like a Tickle Time
to make you feel like new,
so let's all get together
and we'll gitchy-gitchy goo.
GOO BOP. GITCHY GOO BOP...
GITCHY-GITCHY GOO, GITCHY GOO.
Tickle 1, tickle 2. *GITCHY GOO BOP.*
Tickle PINK,
tickle BLUE. *GITCHY-GITCHY.*
Tickle back, tickle forth.
Tickle east and tickle north.
Tickle south, tickle west.

We think Tickle Time's the best.
Tickle smooth, tickle rough,
Tickle till you've had enough.

Gitchy-gitchy goo, gotta gitchy-gitchy goo, gotta...

Now everybody's had enough.
Everybody's had enough.

Gitchy-gitchy goo, gotta gitchy-gitchy goo, gotta...

We said, "Everybody's had enough."
HEY, EVERYBODY'S HAD ENOUGH!
Gitchy-gitchy goo, gitchy...
STOP STOP STOP!
(Phew.)

GOO.

Dinosaur Round

With infinite exasperation

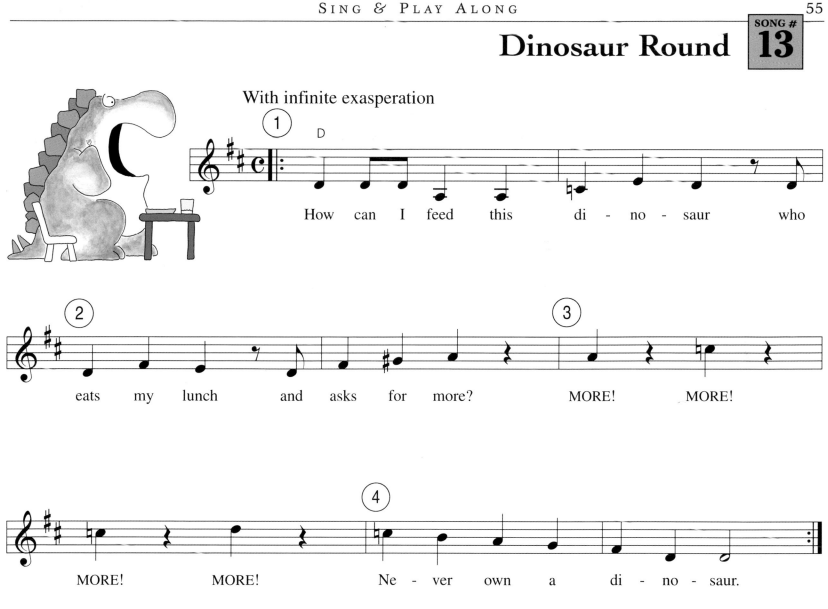

How can I feed this di - no - saur who eats my lunch and asks for more? MORE! MORE! MORE! MORE! Ne - ver own a di - no - saur.

"MORE!"

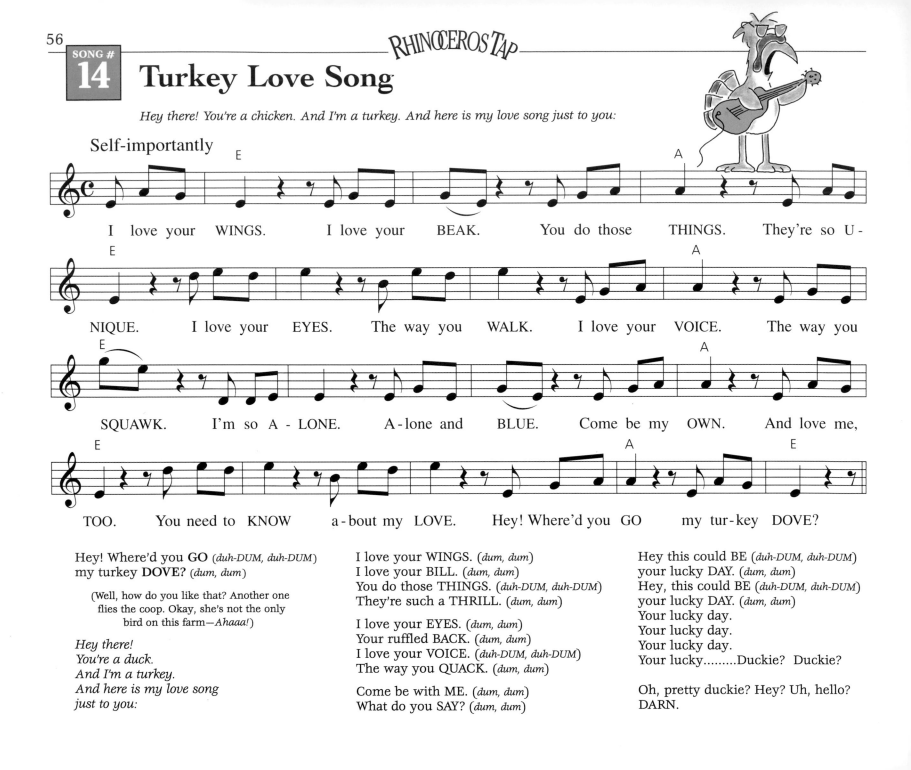

SONG # 14 Turkey Love Song

Hey there! You're a chicken. And I'm a turkey. And here is my love song just to you:

Self-importantly

I love your WINGS. I love your BEAK. You do those THINGS. They're so U-

NIQUE. I love your EYES. The way you WALK. I love your VOICE. The way you

SQUAWK. I'm so A-LONE. A-lone and BLUE. Come be my OWN. And love me,

TOO. You need to KNOW a-bout my LOVE. Hey! Where'd you GO my tur-key DOVE?

Hey! Where'd you **GO** (*duh-DUM, duh-DUM*)
my turkey **DOVE?** (*dum, dum*)

*(Well, how do you like that? Another one
flies the coop. Okay, she's not the only
bird on this farm—Ahaaa!)*

Hey there!
You're a duck.
And I'm a turkey.
And here is my love song
just to you:

I love your WINGS. (*dum, dum*)
I love your BILL. (*dum, dum*)
You do those THINGS. (*duh-DUM, duh-DUM*)
They're such a THRILL. (*dum, dum*)

I love your EYES. (*dum, dum*)
Your ruffled BACK. (*dum, dum*)
I love your VOICE. (*duh-DUM, duh-DUM*)
The way you QUACK. (*dum, dum*)

Come be with ME. (*dum, dum*)
What do you SAY? (*dum, dum*)

Hey this could BE (*duh-DUM, duh-DUM*)
your lucky DAY. (*dum, dum*)
Hey, this could BE (*duh-DUM, duh-DUM*)
your lucky DAY. (*dum, dum*)
Your lucky day.
Your lucky day.
Your lucky day.
Your lucky.........Duckie? Duckie?

Oh, pretty duckie? Hey? Uh, hello?
DARN.

Little One

Tenderly

Lit-tle One, Lit-tle One, night-time is near-ing. Lit-tle One, Lit-tle One, it's time for sleep.

Lit-tle One, Lit-tle One, stars are ap-pear-ing, sil-ver and gold in the si-lent and deep. The roll of the

ri-ver, the song of the sea, the hush of the dark-en-ing sky,__ the rus-tl-ing for-est, the whis-per-ing wind, the

sound of a soft lul-la-by,__for my Lit-tle One, Lit-tle One, come, let me hold you. Lit-tle One, Lit-tle One,

come here with me. Lit-tle One, Lit-tle One, have-n't I told you you're the best Lit-tle One ev-er could be?

rah! *Yay!!!!* ENCORE!

RAVO! BRAVO! BR

ay! MORE, MO

!!!! ENCORE! ENCOR

BRAVO! BRAVO! B

RE, MORE! *Yay!*

CORE! ENCORE! BRA

/// Hurrah! Hurrah!

Book Credits
& Thank-yous

Will the entire *Rhinoceros Tap* production team at Workman Publishing please come forward now, to receive the applause and gratitude they so emphatically deserve?

EDITOR / DANCE CAPTAIN Suzanne Rafer
DESIGN Paul Hanson
PRODUCTION Elizabeth Gaynor
MANAGEMENT OF ART Harry Schroder
PUBLICITY Kim Hicks
EXECUTIVE PRODUCER Peter Workman

with the cheerful and tireless help of—
Barbie Altorfer, Anne Cherry, Nicki Clendening, Beth Doty, Rick Grossman,
Philip Hoffhines, Elizabeth Johnsboen, Wayne Kirn, Anthony Pedone,
Robyn Schwartz, Max Sentry, Kim Small, Carolan Workman, Katie Workman

Thank you also to Ron Ricketts, Christine Antonsen, Shawn Ricketts,
Wayne Booth, and Andrew Bent at Rammgraph,
for their careful attention to the many subtleties of art reproduction.

Recording Credits
& Thank-yous

FOLD →

are printed on this HANDY CD INSERT!

If you find that your CD wants to go wherever
it is you're going, yet your book prefers to
loll about the house, you can make a
snazzy holder for the CD.
Simply cut where indicated, fold the 2 side flaps
inward, then insert this *plus* your
RHINOCEROS TAP compact disc
into a new, clear plastic CD case,
available wherever fine plastic CD cases are sold.

FOLD →

CUT HERE
VERTICALLY

THANK YOU

RHINOCERIOUSLY TO

LISA BIAGINI
BETH ANDRIEN
JAMIE McEWAN

AND TO
Kathleen Sherrill
FOR COORDINATING THE UNCOORDINATED

FOR ENCOURAGEMENT & STEADFAST FRIENDSHIP

Matt Biagini
Caitlin McEwan, Keith Boynton
Devin McEwan, Darcy Boynton
Rachel, John, and Katie Ford
Jeanne Boynton, Jood & Rick
Pam & John, Laurie & Carl
Jane & Mark Capecelatro
Jenifer & Mark Clarke
Robin Corey
Randy Dwenger & Steve Callahan
Sarah Getz, Laura Linney
Bill & Sue Kirber
Brian Mann & Renée Katz
Jacquelyn Tintle, Linda Epstein
Sam & Ellen Posey
Nora & Bob Rivkin
Bob & Joanne Sohrweide
Susan Spano, Christine Stevens
Bevan & Alinda Stanley

All lead vocals by
ADAM BRYANT

All instruments played by
MICHAEL FORD

Recording/mixing engineers
CHRIS TERGESEN
at The Hit Factory, NYC

MICHAEL FORD
at MFA Studios, Malvern, PA

Album mastered by
CHRIS GEHRINGER
at The Hit Factory and Sterling Sound, NYC

PRODUCED BY SANDRA BOYNTON

All lyrics by SANDRA BOYNTON
All arrangements by
The Lone Arranger, MICHAEL FORD

Music by—
Rhinoceros Tap FORD
O, Lonely Peas FORD
Bad Babies BOYNTON/FORD
The Crabby Song
      BOYNTON/FORD/McEWAN
Perfect Piggies FORD
Tropical Sand BOYNTON/FORD
So Long, Doggies FORD
The Shortest Song in the Universe FORD
Horns to Toes FORD
Barnyard Dance FORD
I Love You More
      Than Cheese BOYNTON/FORD
Tickle Time FORD
Dinosaur Round FORD
Turkey Love Song
      BOYNTON/FORD/BRYANT
Little One BOYNTON

SPECIAL THANKS TO

The Ensoniq Corporation
The Adam's Mark Hotel, Philadelphia
Mel Shulman at Impact
Tri-Arts Theatre

FOR GENERAL GOOD WORK

David Allender
F. M. Alexander
Fred Astaire

Barnyard Dance is based on Sandra Boynton's board book
      published by Workman Publishing

Horns to Toes is based on Sandra Boynton's board book
      published by Simon & Schuster

Design: Paul Hanson & Sandra Boynton

© and ℗ 1996, 2004 Sandra Boynton

ALL RIGHTS RESERVED

Little One © S K Boynton Music (ASCAP)
All other songs © Boynton/Ford Music (ASCAP)

Please visit our web site, such as it is:
WWW.BOYNTONSONGS.COM

Published, and sold as a book/CD set, by
WORKMAN PUBLISHING COMPANY, INC. • NEW YORK, N.Y.

The end.

Thank you.